To order additional copies of this book, contact:
Xlibris
0800-056-3182
www.xlibrispublishing.co.uk
Orders@ Xlibrispublishing.co.uk

ISBN: Softcover   978-1-9845-9006-0
         EBook   978-1-9845-9007-7

Print information available on the last page

Rev. date: 07/22/2019

The Magical Treasure Hunt

by Domas Cepskis

One sunny morning King Jack and his horse Endor were enjoying their breakfast in their beautiful garden. The sun was out, the birds were singing and everyone around was very happy.

Jack saw a bottle in his MAGIC rainbow river. He jumped in the river and took the bottle out. It looked very old and interesting.

The King looked closely at the bottle and saw something IN IT ...

He opened the bottle...

AND...there inside was a TREASURE MAP!

The map was very old and it was hard to read.

W ithout a second thought King Jack packed his bags, took his horse Endor and flew off to meet his ship and his crew.

Endor was a beautiful horse with ears so BIG they allowed him to fly.

"Lets the adventure begin!!! – Jack said as he looked at the map.

On the map he saw an ISLAND. The island was far, far away across three oceans and hundreds of HILLS.

His beautiful ship was waiting at the beach. The ship was called "The Friendly Shark" and it was looked after by TEN of his best knights.

They sailed for many days and many nights to get to Treasure Island.

One very stormy night they met some very dangerous PIRATES.

The pirates were very messy. The pirate ship was so untidy that it could barely move.

The Pirates were not friendly at all. They started a BATTLE and wanted to take King Jack's Ship.

However, King Jack's crew were well prepared for battle and were ready to fight back.

Both ships fired cannonballs at the same time...

BOOOOOOOOOOOOOOOOOOM!!!

There was lots of noise. The noise was so loud that it hurt Jack's ears. Endor was so scared. His ears were so big and sensitive that he could even hear the tiniest of ANTS talk...

The cannonballs crashed into each other and fell down into deep blue sea.

NO ONE WAS HURT.

The Pirates turned around and sailed far away back to their Pirate LAND.

King Jack was very proud of his crew. They had a big celebration with lots of cakes and TREATS.

Endor had lots of apples and even a slice of cake. He was the HAPPIEST horse ever.

After all the celebrations and good night's sleep, King Jack, Endor and their crew reached Treasure Island.

Jack and Endor rushed onto the island excited to look around for the promised Treasure.

The crew stayed on the ship but they wished them the best of LUCK.

The friends landed safely. On the island, much to their surprise, they met Mr. Pink and Mr. Beard.

Mr. Pink and Mr. Beard were a pig and goat who had lived there since their ship had sunk. They had survived the shipwreck and lived on the island ever since safe and happy. They even had a tiny little house there and plenty coconuts and BANANAS to eat.

They were very HAPPY to see Jack and Endor arrive on their island.

Jack explained the whole story to Mr. Pink and Mr. Beard and they all joined together to search for the EXCITING treasure.

They walked and walked, around and around, up and down until suddenly they saw big red X hiding in a big bush. They were lucky to see it as there were lots of big palm trees around it. Luckily there was a SHOVEL hidden in bush too.

The gang began to dig a big hole. They dug deeper and deeper. Very deep down and they discovered a very old treasure CHEST.

King Jack tried to open it but had no luck. It was locked with some very big locks.

They made a PLAN to create some wooden keys using a piece of ship.

Finally they opened the treasure chest and couldn't believe what they found!

There in the Treasure chest lay lots of jewels, diamonds, pearls, euros and dollars.

They were all very happy...and very RICH!

Mr. Pink, Mr. Beard, King Jack, Endor and all the ship's crew became the BEST of friends. The animals decided to leave Treasure Island and head back to Jack's Kingdom with their new FRIENDS.

They became the happiest pig and goat EVER.

It took them a few weeks of sailing to finally get home to King Jack's beautiful kingdom complete with castle, MAGIC rainbow river and forest FULL OF LIFE.

They were all really HAPPY and so they had a big PARTY.

All the villagers were invited.

The Kings from all the other countries came too.

They feasted on cakes, popcorns and pizza. They drank lots of drinks. So many cupcakes were made.

Everyone celebrated until morning.

THEY ALL LIVED HAPPILY EVER AFTER.

THE END.

Printed in the United States
By Bookmasters